the CLASS ARTIST

G. BRIAN KARAS

Greenwillow Books
An Imprint of HarperCollinsPublishers

For our dear
and artful friend Harvard

This book would not be a book without the push and pull of
my agent and friend, Paige, the always present support of my editor, Virginia,
and the tireless efforts of everyone at Greenwillow, especially Ava and Sylvie.
Thank you all!

The Class Artist. Copyright © 2001 by G. Brian Karas. All rights reserved.
Printed in Singapore by Tien Wah Press. www.harperchildrens.com

The artwork was prepared with gouache, an opaque watercolor, mixed with acrylic medium and pencil.
The text type is Franklin Gothic Book.

Library of Congress Cataloging-in-Publication Data: Karas, G. Brian. The class artist / by G. Brian Karas.
  p. cm. "Greenwillow Books." Summary: Despite the trouble he has at first working on art projects
at school, Fred develops into the class artist.
ISBN 0-688-17814-6 (trade). ISBN 0-688-17815-4 (lib. bdg.)
[1. Artists—Fiction. 2. Schools—Fiction.] I. Title.   PZ7.K1296 Cl 2001   [E]—dc21   00-048439

1 2 3 4 5 6 7 8 9 10 First Edition

The first day of school wasn't Fred's best day.
"I wish I could draw," said Fred when
he got home. "Everyone says I can't
even draw a straight line."
"Who's everyone?" asked his sister, Martha.
"Frances," said Fred.

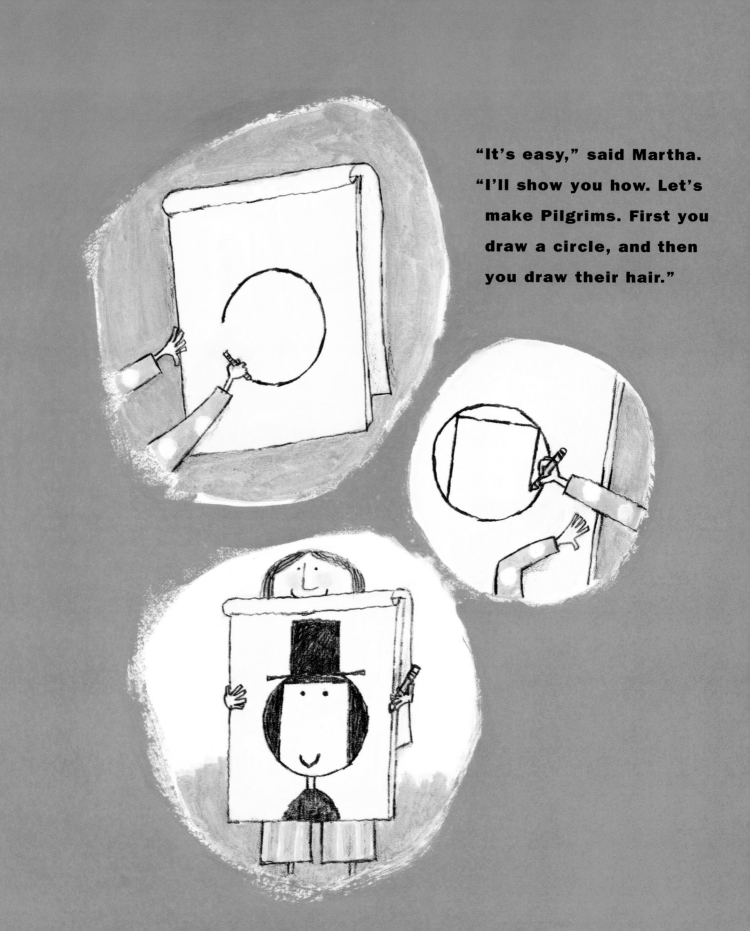

"It's easy," said Martha. "I'll show you how. Let's make Pilgrims. First you draw a circle, and then you draw their hair."

Fred caught on quickly.
"See, I told you it was
easy," said Martha.
"It *is* easy!" said Fred.
Drawing became Fred's
favorite thing to do.

artist

But then one Monday . . .

"Boys and girls," said the teacher, "you have an entire week for your next art project. You can make anything you want, and at the end of the week you will have a chance to share your work with the class."

I'm going to draw my dog doing tricks.

I'm going to draw a big building.

Everyone got right to work.

"What are you going to draw, more Pilgrims?"
asked Frances.
Fred didn't hear her. He was thinking hard.

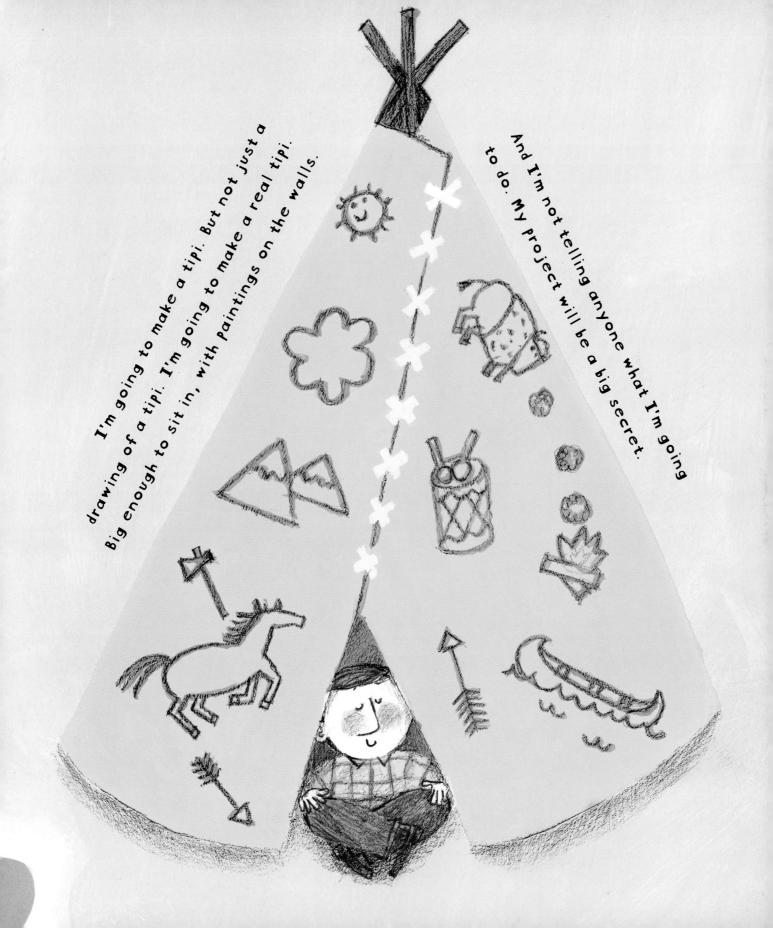

I'm going to make a tipi. But not just a drawing of a tipi. I'm going to make a real tipi. Big enough to sit in, with paintings on the walls.

And I'm not telling anyone what I'm going to do. My project will be a big secret.

"May I have extra-large sheets of paper?" Fred asked
the teacher. He found an unoccupied corner where he
could be left alone.
Frances raised her hand. "Fred is being sneaky."

Fred soon found out that he didn't know how to make his tipi. He didn't know how to curve the paper to make the tipi look real. He didn't know how to cut the paper or where to glue or how to make it stand up. But he still had lots of time to work it out.

No one could wait until sharing time
at the end of the week.
Except Fred.

Look at my drawing of when I got stuck up in the tree.

"Let's see your drawing, Fred," said Frances.

"Top secret," said Fred.

But the week was going by and Fred still couldn't figure out how to make his tipi.

I can't ask the teacher for help, he thought.

I can't ask *anyone* for help, even Martha. That will spoil the big surprise at the end of the week.

THURSDAY

But the end of the week was tomorrow. Fred was
almost out of time. He walked home from school and
thought as hard as he could about how to make his tipi.
He could still do it. He *would* do it!

"Okay, girls and boys," said the teacher.

"Let's take out our work for all to see."

DAY

It was sharing time,
and Fred had nothing to share.

"Why do you keep clearing your throat?"
Frances asked Fred. "Why do you keep
feeling your heartbeat?"
The teacher was getting close.

Fred quickly drew a little tipi on a piece
of white paper and cut it out.

Maybe no one will notice its small size.

It looks kind of okay.

The teacher came up to Fred and looked at his little tipi.
She held it up. "Is this the best you could do
after an entire week?" she asked him with surprise.
Fred thought about telling her all about his big plan
for his big tipi, but he knew it wouldn't do any good.

I give up being an artist.

When it was circle time,

Fred didn't sit in the circle.

He sat alone and stared at his tipi.

"Why don't you join us in the circle?"
asked his teacher.
"I don't feel so well," Fred mumbled back.
"Hmm," she said. "Why don't you draw
a picture of how you feel?"

That would be easy, thought Fred.
He got one of the big sheets of paper and
drew a black cloud. It looked like smoke.
It gave him an idea.

Fred glued his tipi
next to the black
cloud. It looks like
my tipi is on fire.
Good, he thought.

But it didn't *feel* good to Fred. He liked his tipi.

He had worked so hard on his tipi all week.

And now it made him sad to see it go up in smoke.

Fred got to work.

"Wow," said Frances.
"I wish I could draw
like you."
"Thanks," said Fred.

And that was the beginning of
Fred's career as class artist.